Tudley
Didn't Know

Written and Illustrated by John Himmelman

Thanks to James White,
Associate Director, Land & Biodiversity Management of The Delaware Nature Society
and Co-author of *Amphibians & Reptiles of Delmarva*,
and to Jim D'Angelo, Director of the Sterling Nature Center
for checking the accuracy of the "For Creative Minds" section.

Publisher's Cataloging-In-Publication Data

Himmelmann, John.
Tudley didn't know / written and illustrated by John Himmelmann.

1 v. (unpaged) : ill. (chiefly col.) ; 26 cm.

Summary: Tudley, a pond-living painted turtle, adopts other animals' behaviors -- simply because he
doesn't know he can't! He flies like a bird, sings like a katydid, hops like a frog, and glows like a firefly.
Includes "For Creative Minds" section with fun facts and crafts.
ISBN: 978-0-9764943-6-2 (hardcover)
ISBN: 978-1-934359-04-4 (pbk.)

1. Painted turtle--Juvenile fiction. 2. Animal behavior--Juvenile fiction. 3. Turtles--Fiction.
4. Animal behavior--Fiction. I. Title.

PZ7.H45 Tu 2006
[Fic]   2005921143

Printed in China

Sylvan Dell Publishing
976 Houston Northcutt Blvd., Suite 3
Mt. Pleasant, SC 29464

Tudley was a young turtle who lived in a great big pond. He and all the other turtles liked to spend the warm summer afternoons lying in the sun. It was nice being a turtle in the sun.

One afternoon Tudley stretched out on a rock and watched a hummingbird build its nest. The bird dropped a piece of lichen and it landed next to Tudley.

"I'll get that," said Tudley. He picked up the lichen and flew up to the nest.

"Here you go," he said to the hummingbird.

"What did you just do?" asked the bird.

"I brought you your lichen," said the turtle.

"But turtles can't fly," said the bird.

"They can't?" said Tudley. "I didn't know that."

He looked down at the shocked faces of turtles below. "Did you know that turtles can't fly?" he called down. They all just nodded.

That night as Tudley was resting from a long day of flying from here to there and there to here, he watched the fireflies glowing in the dark. Then he heard a tiny little "plip." A firefly had fallen into the water beside him. Tudley fished him out.

"Thank you," said the firefly, "but now I am too wet to fly and everyone will be going home soon."

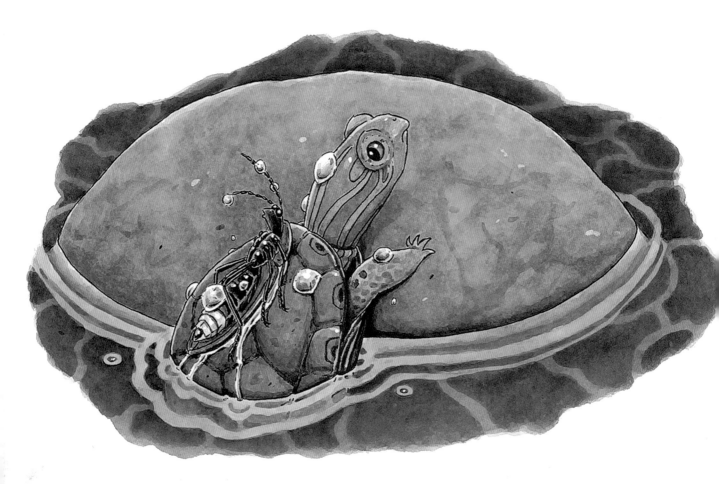

"I will call for help," said Tudley. He lifted his tail in the air and made it glow bright green. "Blink, blink, blink," went his tail as he signaled to the other fireflies.

One of them landed next to the turtle. "How did you do that?" he asked.

"Do what?" asked Tudley.

"Make your tail glow," said the firefly. "Turtles can't make their tails glow."

"They can't?" said Tudley. "I didn't know that."

He looked at the other turtles who had gathered around him. Their mouths hung wide open.

"Did you know our tails don't glow?" he asked. They all just nodded their heads.

The next morning, a tadpole swam up to Tudley.
"Look," said the tadpole. "I'm growing feet!"

But then the tadpole looked sad. "I wish I could show my mom," he said.

"Where is she?" asked Tudley.

"Out hopping in the meadow," said the tadpole.

"I will find her," said Tudley.

He went to the meadow and found the tadpole's mother.
Tudley hopped up along side her. "Come back to the pond and
see your tadpole," he said. "He's got legs!"

"Oh my!" said the frog.

As the two of them hopped back toward the pond, the frog
looked over at the Tudley and said, "you are a special dear,
aren't you?"

"Why?" asked Tudley.

"Turtles can't hop," she said.

"They can't?" said Tudley. "I didn't know that."

"Did you know that turtles can't hop?" shouted Tudley as he hopped up to the other turtles. The other turtles blinked and then slowly sunk under the water.

That evening, Tudley heard some katydids singing in the trees. Each called from the highest branch it could find. Tudley liked their music and decided to join them. He flew up to the tallest tree at the edge of the meadow.

"How do you make that beautiful sound?" he called to one of the katydids.

"We rub our wings together," he answered.

I do not have wings, he thought, but I can rub my arms together. Soon he was singing like the katydids.

"Hey, turtles can't sing," a katydid shouted.

"They can't? I didn't know that," said Tudley. "Did you know that turtles can't sing?" he called down to the other turtles.

Oh, I forgot, he thought. *The turtles aren't even here—they are back at the pond.* Suddenly, Tudley lost his balance.

He fell from the tree and landed upside-down on a rock.

"Help!" called Tudley.

Tudley tried to fly off the rock, but he could not fly upside-down.

He tried to hop off the rock, but his legs just waved in the air. Tudley was frightened.

He saw the fireflies glowing in the air. It gave him an idea.
He blinked his tail to call for help.

Then Tudley felt something land on his chest. It was the firefly he had saved a while back.

"I can't get down. If I tip over, I will fall and hurt myself," said Tudley.

"I saw you needed help and brought some friends," he said.

Just then the mother frog and the hummingbird appeared.

But the frog, the firefly, and the bird were afraid to move him.

"I will get the older turtles," said the firefly. "They will know what to do."

Tudley spent the night on the rock waiting for the slow-moving turtles.

He was still scared, but the frog, katydids and bird kept him company.

Morning came and Tudley still didn't know what to do.

"Hey Tudley, what are you doing up there?" called a voice from below. The turtles had arrived.

"I am stuck!" yelled Tudley. "Please help me!"

"We can't get up there!" cried the turtles.

"What should I do?" screamed Tudley.

"Tuck into your shell!" said the turtles.
"How do I do that?" asked Tudley.
"Just pull in your head and feet!" yelled the turtles.
Tudley pulled his head and feet inside his shell.

"Now what?" he called from inside his shell.
"Rock back and forth," yelled the turtles.
"I will fall and get hurt!" cried Tudley.
"Your shell will protect you," said the turtles.

Tudley rocked back and forth.

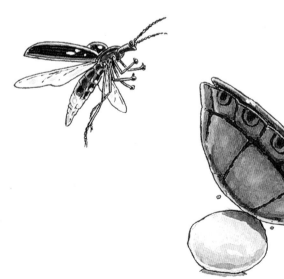

He slipped off the top of the rock and rolled all the way down.

The turtles all gathered around young Tudley.
"Are you okay?" they asked. Tudley poked his head, and then his feet, back out of his shell.

"I didn't know I could do that!" he laughed. As Tudley flew away, some of the other turtles began to wonder . . .

For Creative Minds

Painted Turtles

Tudley is a painted turtle. All turtles are **reptiles**. Reptiles have scaly skin, breathe air, and usually lay eggs. When a reptile hatches, it looks like a miniature version of the adult who laid the egg.

Reptiles are "**cold-blooded**," which means their bodies are warmed or chilled by the air or water around them. Painted turtles love to bask in the sun to get warm. Sometimes they lie with their arms and legs spread out (almost as if they are trying to fly). It takes them a while to warm up.

The shell offers a turtle protection, and a painted turtle can tuck its head, legs, and tail inside of it. Some turtles, like the box turtle, can completely close its shell. A sea turtle cannot pull in its head or flippers at all.

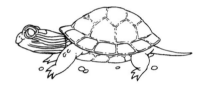

Ruby-throated Hummingbirds

There are 21 different kinds of hummingbirds in the United States. The bird in this story is a Ruby-throated hummingbird, the only hummingbird found in the northeastern United States. Males have shiny red feathers on their throats. They flash the bright colors to attract females. Their nests are often built near or over water and are made from spider webs, thistle, and dandelion down with the outside covered in lichen. Hummingbirds feed on nectar from flowers. They sip the sweet juice with a long tongue.

If you would like to see them up close, you can buy a hummingbird feeder. Hang the feeder near a window (so you can watch from inside). Fill the feeder with sugar water.

Here's how you make it: with the help of an adult mix 1 part sugar and 4 parts water. Boil the water and then mix in the sugar. Let it cool. This can be stored for up to two weeks in your refrigerator. Feeders should be cleaned about every 3 days during warm weather to prevent spoiling of the sugar water.

Fireflies

Fireflies are not flies, but beetles. They are also called "lightning bugs." Both names call attention to the fact that they glow. Not only do most adults blink with a bright, yellow-green light, but the larvae and eggs can glow as well. Turn off the outdoor lights on a warm summer night and watch their show. You will notice some blinking in the air and some on the ground. The ones in the air are usually males who are trying to get the females to notice them. The females stay on the ground and flash their lights when they see a male they like. The male sees her signal and flies down to her.

Leopard Frogs

Leopard frogs are **amphibians**. The word amphibian means "two lives." One part of that animal's life is spent in the water. The other part is spent on land. When an animal changes form as it grows, it is called **metamorphosis**.

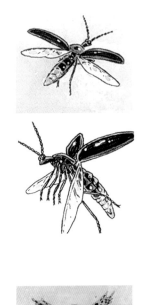

Frogs begin as eggs. The eggs hatch into **tadpoles**, or **pollywogs**. Tadpoles breathe under water through gills. They eat algae, dead plants, and animals. Back legs appear in time. Over the next few weeks the front legs appear. The tadpole grows larger and looks more and more like a frog. The tail slowly gets absorbed into the body, helping to feed the young amphibian while it is changing from a water-breathing animal to an air-breathing animal.

When the new **froglet** leaves the water, it still has a little stump of a tail left. It spends a few weeks around the water as it is growing up. If it is a leopard frog, it will then hop off to the nearest grassy meadow but will return to the water to mate and lay eggs.

True Katydids

The katydid in this story is a True Katydid. These insects are related to grasshoppers but they live up in the trees. They look like the leaves they live in and feed upon. This helps to keep them hidden from hungry birds and other animals.

The males call all night long in the summer and fall. The females call, too, but not as much. The sound of a true Katydid's call is what gave all katydids their name. Some say it sounds like, "Katy-did...... katy-did." *You can make a scratching sound similar to a Katydid by scraping a fingernail over a comb.*

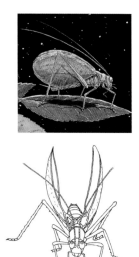

Make a hopping Tudley!

Copy, trace, or download (www.SylvanDellPublishing.com) the three figures. Color in the top shell (**carapace**) and the bottom shell (**plastron**). Cut out the figures. Fold the strip of paper to make a spring. Tape or glue one end of the folded paper to the top of Tudley and one end to the bottom. Give his shell a tap and watch him hop!

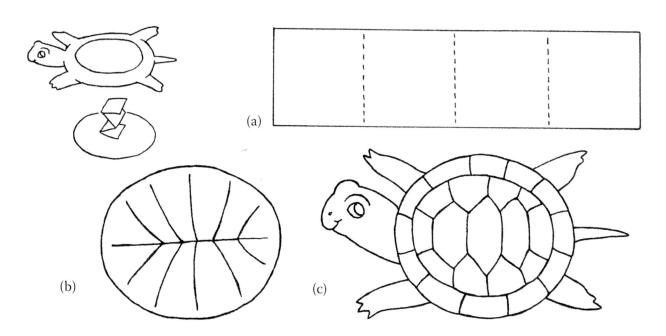

(a)

(b)

(c)

Food for Thought: *Would a turtle really be able to hop? Why or why not?*
Creative Sparks: *Draw a picture of or write a story about an animal that borrows other animals' behaviors or adaptations.*